To Emilia, with love

Special thanks to
Rachel Elliot

ORCHARD BOOKS
338 Euston Road, London NW1 3BH
Orchard Books Australia
Level 17/207 Kent Street, Sydney, NSW 2000
A Paperback Original

First published in 2014 by Orchard Books

A CIP catalogue record for this book is available
from the British Library.

ISBN 978 1 40833 147 7

1 3 5 7 9 10 8 6 4 2

Printed in Great Britain

The paper and board used in this paperback are natural recyclable
products made from wood grown in sustainable forests. The
manufacturing processes conform to the environmental regulations
of the country of origin.

Orchard Books is a division of Hachette Children's Books,
an Hachette UK company

www.hachette.co.uk

Josie
the Jewellery-Making Fairy

by Daisy Meadows

ORCHARD

www.rainbowmagic.co.uk

The Fairyland
Palace

Sara Sketchley's
house

Bridge

Maze

Park

Rainspell
Island

Carys's
Jewellery
Shop

Beach and
Promenade

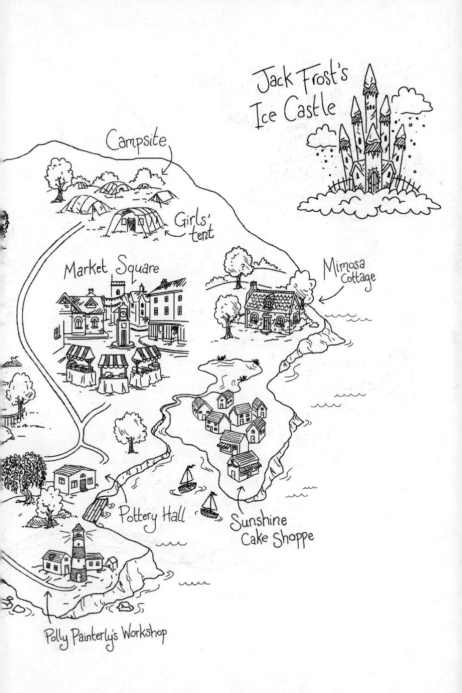

Jack Frost's
Ice Castle

Campsite

Girls'
tent

Market Square

Mimosa
Cottage

Pottery Hall

Sunshine
Cake Shoppe

Polly Painterly's Workshop

Jack Frost's Spell

I'm a wonderful painter, you must have heard of me,
Marvel at my amazing artistic ability!
With palette, brush and paints in hand,
I'll be the most famous artist in the land!

The Magical Crafts Fairies can't stop me,
I'll steal their magic and then you'll see
That everyone, whatever the cost,
Will want a painting by Jack Frost!

Contents

Golden Seashells

Rachel Walker sat up and yawned,
then smiled as she remembered where
she was. It was early in the morning,
but the warmth of the sun was already
soaking through the canvas of her tent.
She looked across at her best friend Kirsty
Tate, who was still curled up in her
sleeping bag. So far their stay on Rainspell
Island had been full of adventure.

"I wonder what today will bring," she whispered to herself.

Rachel leaned back on her pillow and thought about all the things that had happened since they arrived. It was Crafts Week on the island, and so far the girls had tried pottery, drawing and sewing. There were plenty more crafts left to try, as well as a competition and exhibition at the end of the week. Things had got even more exciting when they met Kayla the Pottery Fairy. Rachel and Kirsty were secret friends with all the fairies. Now, as well as enjoying their spring holiday on their favourite island, they were also in the middle of a magical adventure!

Kirsty stirred in her sleep and turned over. Rachel leaned over and unzipped the tent flap. Sunlight spilled into the tent, turning everything golden. Kirsty yawned and opened her eyes.

"Good morning," she said, stretching her arms. "I've been having a lovely dream. I think I sleep better in the tent than in the bed and breakfast!"

Kirsty's family were staying at a little
B&B in the village, and Rachel's family
were camping. The girls had decided to
have alternate sleepovers at each place
all through the week, and it was turning
out to be a lot of fun.

"I think I can hear Mum making the
breakfast," said Rachel, wriggling out of
her sleeping bag. "Come
on, I'm starving!"

The girls got
dressed and pulled
on their sandals.

"What crafts
would you like
to do today,
Rachel?"
asked Kirsty.

"Well, you

know it's my mum's birthday today,"
Rachel said. "It'd be great to make
something to give to her later at
the party."

Mr Walker had organised a surprise
party for his wife, and the girls could
hardly wait. Just then there was a tap on
the tent flap.

"Come in!" said Rachel and
Kirsty together.

Mr Walker came into
the tent and put his
finger to his lips. He
looked very excited.

"I just want
to show you the
present I've got
for your mum," he
whispered to Rachel. "I

had them handmade by Carys
Silver, who runs the jewellery shop
on the seafront."

He held out a tiny velvet box, and
Rachel took it. She opened the
lid and drew in her
breath. Sitting on
a bed of ivory silk
was a pair of gold
earrings, shaped
like seashells.

"They're
beautiful," she
said in a soft voice.

"Really lovely," Kirsty agreed.

Rachel picked up one of the earrings,
but then something awful happened.
The seashell fell away from the loop of
the earring. It was broken!

"I'm sorry!" cried Rachel, feeling very guilty. "I was trying to be careful!"

"It wasn't your fault," said Mr Walker, examining the earrings. "Look, they're both broken. It must have somehow happened while the box was in my pocket."

He sounded upset, and Rachel gave him a big hug.

"Don't worry, Dad," she said.
"I've got an idea. Carys Silver is
running a jewellery-making workshop
in her shop, and we could go down
there and make something for Mum's
birthday ourselves."

"That's a really good idea," Kirsty
said, giving Mr Walker a reassuring
smile. "We can take the earrings back to
be fixed at the same time."

Mr Walker agreed, and then they
heard Mrs Walker's voice.

"Breakfast's ready," she called. "Come
on, everyone!"

They all hurried out of the tent and
filled their plates with bacon, eggs, beans
and tomatoes. The girls wished Mrs
Walker a happy birthday and ate their
breakfast as fast as they could.

"What's the hurry?" asked Mrs Walker with a laugh.

"We're just keen to get to the crafts workshop in town," said Rachel. "Come on, Kirsty, let's go!"

The girls waved goodbye and hurried off before Mrs Walker could ask them what sort of crafts they were going to be doing. They didn't want her to guess that they were making jewellery for her birthday!

Scattered Pearls

The girls ran down through the
buttercup-filled fields towards the village.
The sea stretched out in front of them,
blue and sparkling. A light breeze was
lifting spray from the tips of the waves.

"Wouldn't it be wonderful to live
here all year round?" said Kirsty as they
reached the village.

"Maybe," said Rachel. "But I love coming here for holidays – it makes it extra special when we only have a few days on the island."

The girls linked arms when they reached the main street. There were already lots of people strolling in and out of the gift shops and taking photographs of the quaint little buildings. Kirsty stopped beside a pretty souvenir shop with bunting hanging in the window.

"Look, this shop sells jewellery," she said. "Perhaps we could get some ideas to inspire us."

The girls peered at the jewellery display, but they weren't very impressed.

"That necklace is damaged," said Rachel, pointing to a chipped pendant on a silver chain. "And all the bracelets are turned around the wrong way so we can't see them."

"Let's try the next shop," Kirsty suggested.

But the next shop's jewellery display was even more disappointing. There were a lot of broken brooches, and the gold watches looked dull and unpolished. In every shop the girls tried, all the jewellery was ruined.

"The strange thing is that all the other souvenirs in the shops look so clean and well-looked-after," said Rachel.

Kirsty glanced into the nearest shop. Apart from a jar of tarnished silver rings, the window display was bright and colourful, with lots of wooden toys, hand-painted plates and colourful ornaments.

"Yes, that *is* odd," she said in a

thoughtful voice. "Rachel, do you think that Jack Frost and his goblins might have something to do with this?"

"I bet you're right," said Rachel. "I'm sure that the shops here wouldn't usually have broken jewellery on display."

On their first day on Rainspell Island, Kayla the Pottery Fairy had fluttered out of a clay pot and whisked them off to Fairyland for the grand opening of the fairies' Magical Crafts Week. The Magical Crafts Fairies had shown Kirsty and Rachel their magical objects, which made sure that arts and crafts were fun for everyone. But after King Oberon and Queen Titania announced that they would choose the best crafts to decorate their Fairyland Palace, everything went wrong.

Jack Frost and his pesky goblins had thrown paint-filled balloons into the crowd, splattering everyone with bright green paint. Then they snatched the magical objects from the Magical Crafts Fairies and disappeared to the human world. Jack thought that he was the greatest artist ever, and he had stolen the objects so that no one could ever be better than him.

"So far, we've helped Kayla the Pottery Fairy, Annabelle the Drawing Fairy and Zadie the Sewing Fairy to get their magical objects back," said Kirsty, thinking back over the last few days.

"But there are still four more objects to find," said Rachel. "We have to keep looking, or the fun of arts and crafts will be gone forever."

"Yes," said Kirsty with a groan, "here and in Fairyland."

At the end of the village's main street, the road widened and led down to the seafront. As the girls walked onto the promenade, they saw a lady on her hands and knees. It was Artemis Johnson, the organiser of Crafts Week, and she looked very upset.

"Artie, are you hurt?" called Rachel, hurrying over to her.

"No, I'm fine," said Artie. "But my pearl necklace just broke, and the pearls have rolled all over the promenade! How will I ever find them all?"

Jinxed Jewellery

"We'll help!" said the girls at once.

In a moment all three of them were crawling around the promenade on their hands and knees. The pearls had rolled into all sorts of cracks and crevices, but Rachel and Kirsty soon found them.

"Goodness me, you must have amazing eyesight," said Artie as Rachel handed her the last pearl.

The girls exchanged secret smiles.
After all, they were used to spotting tiny
fairies! Artie carefully put the pearls in
her bag with the broken string.

"I'll ask Carys Silver to mend it
for me," she went on. "She's a
wonderful jeweller."

"We're on our way
to her shop now,"
said Kirsty. "Shall
we go together?"

"That would be
lovely," said Artie.

They walked
along the
promenade
together,
enjoying the soft
summer breeze.

"Are you having fun on Rainspell?" asked Artie.

"We love it here," said Rachel with a big smile. "Actually this is where we first became friends."

Artie was about to reply when a loud noise from the beach caught her attention. Several boys in large green sunhats were messing around at the edge of the water, trying to push each other in. They were shouting and giggling at the tops of their voices.

"What a racket," said Artie with a frown. "Why are they making so much noise?"

"They must have already been to the jewellery workshop," said Kirsty. "They're wearing every kind of jewellery I can imagine!"

The boys had strings of beaded
necklaces dangling around their necks.
They were wearing so many bracelets
that you could hardly see their arms, and
there were even beaded charms dangling
from their sunhats.

The boys stopped pushing each other
around and started picking shells up
from the beach and putting them into
a bucket.

"Oh dear, collecting seashells isn't
allowed on Rainspell Island any more,"

said Artie, peering across the sand at them. "We're trying really hard to preserve the nature of the seaside."

"Maybe we should all go and tell them," Rachel suggested.

But they had only taken a few steps towards the boys when there was a loud, angry squawk from above. A large seagull flew directly at them!

"Run!" yelled the boys. "Scram!"

They ran off down the beach, shouting all the way. The gull circled above them and then flew back inland.

"Carys's jewellery shop is just up there," said Artie.

She pointed to a little wooden shop overlooking the beach. It was painted sky blue, and the window that looked out to sea reached from the floor all the way up to the ceiling.

"Carys sits in that window to design her jewellery," Artie told the girls. "The seashore inspires all her designs."

When Rachel and Kirsty reached the shop, two girls walked out shaking their heads.

"I give up on jewellery-making," said the dark-haired girl.

"Me too," said the redhead. "I'm just not good enough."

Rachel and Kirsty exchanged a worried look. Inside the shop, the jewellery-making workshop didn't seem to be going very well. Beads were rolling all over the floor and string was breaking. Carys was dashing from person to person, trying to sort out each problem, while things kept going wrong all around her.

"Carys, what's happening here?"
exclaimed Artie.

Carys stopped rushing around for a
moment and gave Artie a hug. Then she
ran her fingers through her silvery hair,
making it stand up on end.

"It's a total disaster," she said.
"Everything is going wrong today. I
don't know what to do!"

"I'm sorry to hear that," said Artie. "I came over to ask you to fix a necklace and to bring you two extra students for your workshop. But perhaps I should come back tomorrow."

"No, I won't hear of it!" said Carys, giving the girls a warm, welcoming smile. "First, let me see this broken necklace."

Artie handed Carys the necklace, and she immediately cut off a length of string from a roll on the worktop.

"This is a five-minute job," she said, patting Artie's arm. "No problem."

But as she spoke, the pearls dropped off the end of the string and rolled away again. Carys groaned and started to kneel down, but Rachel stopped her.

"We'll get them," she said.

It only took a few seconds to gather the pearls.

"Thank you, girls," said Carys, putting the pearls into a little pot. "I'm all fingers and thumbs today. Would you like to have a look around and see what you would like to make? I'll be with you as soon as I have mended Artie's necklace."

"Are you sure you're not too busy?" asked Kirsty.

Things were still going wrong in the jewellery-making workshop, and students holding bits of broken wire and snapped string were waiting to speak to Carys.

"I would love you to join the workshop," said Carys with a smile. "It hasn't been a *total* disaster today – I had a group of boys here earlier who made some spectacular beaded jewellery."

Rachel glanced at Kirsty. It was good news that some people had managed to make nice jewellery. Perhaps Carys's problems had nothing to do with Jack Frost after all.

"The boys even wanted to make jewellery out of seashells," Carys went on. "They got cross when I told them about preserving the nature of the seaside, and they stormed off in a huff."

"I bet they were the boys we saw on the beach," said Artie.

She started to tell Carys about the boys, and the girls wandered off to look around the little shop. It was full of delicate jewellery, all inspired by the beauty of the sea and the shore. Rachel picked up a silver brooch shaped like a starfish.

"I might make a brooch like this," she said. "Isn't it pretty, Kirsty?"

But Kirsty didn't reply. Rachel looked around in surprise, and saw her gazing at a wooden jewellery box on a shelf in the corner. The box was glowing with a faint light, and there was a beautiful painting of a fairy in the centre.

"Rachel, look at the picture!" said Kirsty in an excited whisper. "Shall we open it?"

"Yes, of course!" said Rachel.

Together, the girls lifted the lid of the jewellery box and out fluttered Josie the Jewellery-Making Fairy!

Footprints in the Sand

Josie was wearing a spangled yellow skirt with a wide belt and a peach cropped top. Beautiful beads and pendants dangled around her neck, and pretty bracelets jangled around her wrists. She held out her hands to the girls.

"Rachel and Kirsty, I need your help!"
she gasped. "I have to find my magical
beaded ribbon. Jewellery is in a terrible
mess in the human world and
in Fairyland."

"Of course we'll help you," said
Kirsty. "What does your magical ribbon
look like?"

"It's pink and it has three sparkly beads
on it," said Josie, tucking her chocolate-
brown hair behind her ears. "Until I find
it and take it back to Fairyland, no one
will be able to make jewellery."

Suddenly Rachel had a thought.

"Carys said that the boys who were in
the shop earlier made some wonderful
jewellery," she said. "How could they
have done that?"

"They must have had my magical

ribbon!" Josie exclaimed, clapping her tiny hands. "I knew you would be able to help me! Where are the boys now?"

"When we saw them they were on the beach," said Kirsty. "If we hurry we might catch up with them."

"Good idea," said Rachel. "Just let me give Carys those earrings that need to be repaired."

Josie hid under the brim of Rachel's sunhat, and then the girls hurried over to Carys, who was still trying to mend Artie's necklace. Rachel took the little velvet box out of her pocket and showed her the golden seashell earrings.

"I'll have a look at them as soon as I've finished mending Artie's necklace," Carys promised.

"We've just got to dash out," Kirsty added. "We'll be back soon!"

Carys was too busy to ask them where they were going. The girls hurried onto the beach and looked around, but the boys were nowhere to be seen.

"It'll be easier to search if we're all fairies," said Josie. "Find a place to hide and I'll use my magic!"

The girls noticed a little row of

brightly-coloured beach huts a little further along. One was open, and they darted inside.

Josie fluttered out from under Rachel's sunhat and waved her wand. For a moment all the girls could see was sparkling diamonds, and then they were fluttering in midair beside Josie.

"Come on," said Rachel. "Let's find those boys!"

The three fairies flew out of the
beach hut and over the beach. Almost
immediately, Kirsty spotted lots of large
footprints in the sand.

"Goodness, they almost look like goblin
footprints!" said Rachel.

The fairies followed the trail until they
found the group of boys. They were still
wearing their large green sunhats and
beaded jewellery, and they were building
sandcastles. From their bird's-eye view
the fairies could see something amazing.
The boys had green feet!

"The *boys* are making the footprints,"
said Josie. "How is that possible?"

"Those aren't boys," said Rachel.
"They're goblins!"

At that moment, one of the goblins
started shouting and waving his arms
around. Then he shoved the goblin next
to him, who fell over and squashed a
sandcastle. Soon, all the goblins were
squabbling, pushing each other over and
kicking the sandcastles.

"Let's fly down," said Kirsty. "They're arguing too much to notice us!"

The three fairies fluttered down and hid behind the turrets of a nearby sandcastle. A goblin with a very spotty face picked up a red plastic spade and started digging. Another goblin elbowed him in the ribs and snatched the spade.

"My turn!" he squawked.

He started digging too, but soon a third goblin had grabbed the spade from him.

"Why do they only have one spade?" asked Rachel. "And what are they digging for? They're not picking up shells any more."

"Perhaps they think they'll find buried treasure," said Kirsty.

Suddenly there was a loud squawk, and a seagull landed beside them on the sandcastle.

"Hello!" said Rachel with a smile. "Kirsty, this is the same seagull we saw earlier – the one who scared the goblins away."

The seagull squawked again, and Josie smiled. The girls remembered that all fairies could speak to animals.

"He says hello," Josie told them. "Seagull, do you know what the goblins are doing here on the beach?"

The seagull gave a few more squawks, and Josie turned to the girls.

"He thinks that the goblins have lost something," she said. "They've been looking for ages."

Just then, some beaded charms dropped off one goblin's sunhat. Another goblin's necklace snapped, and the beads scattered across the sand.

"That's odd," said Rachel. "They've got the charm, so their jewellery shouldn't break."

"Oh!" exclaimed Kirsty, opening her eyes wide. "Perhaps the thing they've lost is Josie's magical charm!"

Green
Ice Cream

Their hearts thumping with excitement, the three friends fluttered into the air and spread out.

"Fly low over the beach and look carefully," said Josie. "We've got to find the charm before the goblins do!"

Rachel saw a flash in the sunlight and zoomed down towards it, but it was just a shiny pebble. Kirsty gasped when

she saw something shining down by
the water. But when she flew closer she
realised that it was just a piece of wet
seaweed. Josie was hovering near the
goblins in case they found the charm. She
edged closer to try to see into the hole
they were digging, and then one of the
goblins gave an angry screech.

"A fairy!" he yelled. "There's a fairy
spying on us!"

He kicked sand at Josie, and
some of it went in her eyes.

Unable to see, she flew left and right, trying to get away. Rachel and Kirsty zoomed to her side and pulled her to shelter behind a plastic bucket.

"More fairies!" squawked the goblins. "It's a swarm! Get them!"

But then the fairies heard one of the goblins shout something. The next moment, they were all running off along the beach.

"Why have they gone?" asked Kirsty. "What have they seen?"

While Josie blinked the sand out of her eyes, Kirsty and Rachel peeked around the side of the bucket. In the distance, close to the edge of the water, they could see a special glow. It was obviously something magical.

"That's my ribbon, I'm sure of it!" said Josie, over their shoulders.

"But the goblins have a big head start," Kirsty said with a groan. "We'll never catch them up."

"Then we just have to be cleverer than them," said Rachel. "Quickly, Josie, turn us back into humans and disguise us as ice cream sellers. If there's one thing that we know about the goblins, it's that they're very, very greedy!"

The only thing on the beach was a stripy windbreak, so the fairies hid behind it and Josie waved her wand. Instantly, the girls were human-sized again, and they were wearing white jackets and little white hats. Each of them was holding a tray of green ice creams. They popped out from behind the windbreak, and Josie used her magic to play the sort of tinkling music that ice cream vans use.

"Free ice creams!" called Rachel at the top of her voice. "Get your free ice creams here!"

The goblins stopped in their tracks and turned around. The spotty one was already dribbling.

"We can get the ribbon in a minute," the girls heard one of them say. "There's time to grab an ice cream."

They ran up to Rachel and Kirsty, stumbling over their own feet and pushing each other out of the way.

"Give us our free ice creams *now*!" they shouted.

While Rachel and Kirsty handed out the ice creams, Josie flew down to get her magical ribbon. But just at that moment the spotty goblin turned around, and he saw her flying towards the charm.

"STOP!" he shouted.

He kicked out wildly, and his enormous foot scooped up a large amount of sand. It hit Josie and knocked her sideways.

Another goblin sprinted over to the ribbon and grabbed it.

"Got it!" he squawked, holding it up above his head like a trophy. "Ha ha, little fairy, you're too slow to beat us!"

The goblins cheered and sniggered, their faces now covered in green ice cream. Josie flew back to the girls, her wings drooping.

"I'm never going to get my ribbon back now," she said.

"Maybe we could ask the nice seagull for help," said Kirsty.

She looked up and saw the seagull circling high overhead.

"I've got one ice cream left," said Rachel. "I wonder if he would like some."

They waved at the seagull and he landed beside them. Rachel offered him the ice cream, and while he ate it, Josie explained what had happened.

"Will you help me to get my magical ribbon back?" she asked.

The girls couldn't understand his reply, but he nodded his head and Josie smiled.

"He says yes," she said. "The goblins have been messing up the beach, so he wants them to go home."

The goblins were skipping down the beach, tossing the ribbon between them.

SQUAWWWWK!

The seagull swooped after the goblins, flying so low that he could have pecked their ears.

The goblins cowered and squealed.

"Get off!" they wailed. "Leave us alone!"

The seagull squawked again, and he was so loud that the goblins clapped their hands over their ears and ran.

"Look!" cried Rachel, pointing and jumping up and down.

In their fright, the goblins had dropped the magical ribbon!

Sparkly Surprises

The seagull scooped up the magical ribbon in his beak and flew back to Josie. The beads on the ribbon twinkled as he handed it to her. It immediately shrank to fairy size.

"Thank you!" said Josie. "Now I can put everything right!"

With a wave of her wand, the shells
from the goblins' bucket were returned to
the beach where they belonged. Rachel
and Kirsty's disguises disappeared, and
they were back in their normal clothes
and sunhats once again.

"You have all been wonderful," said
Josie, smiling at Rachel, Kirsty and
the seagull. "Thank you for everything

you have done. Jewellery is safe again
because of you!"

"We were happy to help," said Kirsty.

Rachel nodded and the seagull
squawked in agreement.

"I hope we'll meet again one day,"
said Josie.

She waved goodbye and then
disappeared in a twinkling flash.
The seagull hopped away across the
sand, and Rachel and Kirsty smiled
at each other.

"That's another of the Magical Crafts
Fairies' charms that Jack Frost can't use,"
said Rachel. "Now there are only three
more to find!"

"But first we have to make our presents
for your mum," Kirsty reminded her.
"Come on!"

They ran back to the jewellery shop. This time, it seemed like a very different place. There was a lot of laughter and a buzz of excitement in the workshop. Carys was walking slowly around the tables, checking that everyone was OK. She smiled as the girls sat at an empty table, and came over to see them.

"Things have really calmed down here," she said. "It was a bit of a crazy morning, but now the jewellery-making is going very well. I've even had time to mend your mum's earrings."

She handed Rachel the little velvet box. Inside, the golden seashell earrings were perfect again.

"Thank you so much," said Rachel. "Mum will love them!"

Artie came up to join them and

showed the girls that she was wearing
her pearl necklace.

"Carys mended it beautifully," she said.
"I think she's like a magic fairy, fixing
all the jewellery so fast!"

The girls exchanged a secret smile.
Little did Artie know that magic really
was involved in jewellery-making!

"The trays in front of you contain all

sorts of beads, wires, threads and fixings
for your jewellery," Carys told the girls.
"You can make whatever you like, and
I'll help you if you get stuck. Have fun!"

Looking through the little trays, Rachel
found some beautiful wooden beads.
Each one was painted with a different
type of seashell.

"I think I'll make Mum a necklace
with these beads," she said.

"I'll make a bracelet to match," said
Kirsty, feeling excited. "Then she'll have
a matching set, because the earrings are
seashells too!"

The girls put their heads down and
started to work.

That evening, the girls took Mrs
Walker for a walk along the cliffs while
her surprise party was being prepared.

When they came back to the campsite, Mrs Walker's mouth fell open. Strings of fairy lights were draped from tent to tent. Mr Walker and Mr and Mrs Tate were standing around a glowing campfire, and there was a little pile of presents on the camping table. There was even a big "Happy Birthday" banner! Mrs Tate had baked a cake, and Mr Tate was busy toasting marshmallows. Mrs Walker couldn't believe her eyes.

"Happy birthday!" shouted the girls.

Everyone laughed and hugged Mrs
Walker, who was too surprised to speak.
She blew out the candles on her cake
and then sat down to open her presents.

"What beautiful earrings!" she cried,
putting them on at once. "And a
necklace and bracelet to match. I've
never had such lovely jewellery!"

The girls told her all about making
the necklace and the bracelet. Then Mrs
Tate asked to see the earrings, and Kirsty
and Rachel slipped away to eat their
toasted marshmallows.

"I've got an extra surprise for you,"
said Rachel. "While we were in the
shop, I made you something."

She gave Kirsty a delicate friendship
bracelet in blue, pink and lilac. Kirsty
hugged her and laughed.

"I've got a surprise for you too," she said – pulling out a red, gold and orange friendship bracelet!

"I guess that just shows we were made to be best friends," laughed Rachel.

They tied the bracelets around each other's wrists. Then Kirsty gasped. On each of the friendship bracelets, a  tiny, sparkling fairy bead had appeared.

"They must be a thank-you gift from Josie," said Rachel. "What a wonderful way to end a surprise-filled day!"

The End

Now it's time for Kirsty and Rachel to help…

Violet the Painting Fairy

Read on for a sneak peek…

"We're not far from the lighthouse now, Kirsty," said Rachel. The two girls were walking along the cliff path towards the headland where the Rainspell Island lighthouse stood. "Dad said we can't miss it! I wonder what he meant?"

"We'll soon find out!" Kirsty replied. "I'm so glad we came to Rainspell for another holiday, Rachel. There isn't anywhere else like it in the whole world!"

The girls were spending the spring holiday on Rainspell Island, and they were taking it in turns to stay with

Kirsty's mum and dad at their bed and breakfast one night, and then at the campsite with Rachel's parents the next.

"It's an extra-special holiday because it's Rainspell Crafts Week," Rachel pointed out, "*And* because of our adventures with the Magical Crafts Fairies!"

Read **Violet the Painting Fairy** to find out what adventures are in store for Kirsty and Rachel!

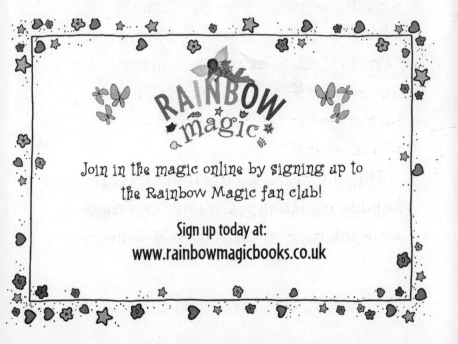

Meet the
Magical Crafts Fairies

Kayla
the Pottery
Fairy

Annabelle
the Drawing
Fairy

Zadie
the Sewing
Fairy

Josie
the Jewellery
Fairy

Violet
the Painting
Fairy

Libby
the Story-Writing
Fairy

Roxie
the Baking
Fairy

Jack Frost has stolen the Magical Crafts Fairies' special
objects. Can Kirsty and Rachel help get them back
before Rainspell Island's Crafts Week is ruined?

www.rainbowmagicbooks.co.uk

Competition!

The Magical Crafts Fairies have created a special
competition just for you!
In the back of each book in the Magical Crafts series there
will be a question for you to answer.
First you need to collect the answer from the back
of each book in the series.
Once you have all the answers, take the first letter from
each one and arrange them to spell a secret word!
When you have the answer, go online and enter!

**Josie the Jewellery-Making Fairy's
magical object is a ribbon.
What three things does it
have on it?**

_ _ _ _ _ _

We will put all the correct entries into a draw and select
a winner to receive a special Rainbow Magic Goody Bag
featuring lots of treats for you and your fairy friends.
You'll also star in a new Rainbow Magic story!

Enter online now at www.rainbowmagicbooks.co.uk

Have you read them all?

The Rainbow Fairies
1. Ruby the Red Fairy ☐
2. Amber the Orange Fairy ☐
3. Saffron the Yellow Fairy ☐
4. Fern the Green Fairy ☐
5. Sky the Blue Fairy ☐
6. Izzy the Indigo Fairy ☑
7. Heather the Violet Fairy ☐

The Weather Fairies
8. Crystal the Snow Fairy ☑
9. Abigail the Breeze Fairy ☐
10. Pearl the Cloud Fairy ☐
11. Goldie the Sunshine Fairy ☐
12. Evie the Mist Fairy ☑
13. Storm the Lightning Fairy ☐
14. Hayley the Rain Fairy ☐

The Party Fairies
15. Cherry the Cake Fairy ☐
16. Melodie the Music Fairy ☐
17. Grace the Glitter Fairy ☐
18. Honey the Sweet Fairy ☐
19. Polly the Party Fun Fairy ☐
20. Phoebe the Fashion Fairy ☐
21. Jasmine the Present Fairy ☐

The Jewel Fairies
22. India the Moonstone Fairy ☐
23. Scarlett the Garnet Fairy ☐
24. Emily the Emerald Fairy ☐
25. Chloe the Topaz Fairy ☐
26. Amy the Amethyst Fairy ☐
27. Sophie the Sapphire Fairy ☐
28. Lucy the Diamond Fairy ☑

The Pet Keeper Fairies
29. Katie the Kitten Fairy ☐
30. Bella the Bunny Fairy ☐
31. Georgia the Guinea Pig Fairy ☐
32. Lauren the Puppy Fairy ☐
33. Harriet the Hamster Fairy ☐
34. Molly the Goldfish Fairy ☐
35. Penny the Pony Fairy ☐

The Fun Day Fairies
36. Megan the Monday Fairy ☐
37. Tallulah the Tuesday Fairy ☐
38. Willow the Wednesday Fairy ☐
39. Thea the Thursday Fairy ☐
40. Freya the Friday Fairy ☑
41. Sienna the Saturday Fairy ☐
42. Sarah the Sunday Fairy ☐

The Petal Fairies
43. Tia the Tulip Fairy ☐
44. Pippa the Poppy Fairy ☐
45. Louise the Lily Fairy ☐
46. Charlotte the Sunflower Fairy ☐
47. Olivia the Orchid Fairy ☐
48. Danielle the Daisy Fairy ☐
49. Ella the Rose Fairy ☐

The Dance Fairies
50. Bethany the Ballet Fairy ☐
51. Jade the Disco Fairy ☐
52. Rebecca the Rock'n'Roll Fairy ☐
53. Tasha the Tap Dance Fairy ☐
54. Jessica the Jazz Fairy ☐
55. Saskia the Salsa Fairy ☐
56. Imogen the Ice Dance Fairy ☐

The Sporty Fairies
57. Helena the Horseriding Fairy ☐
58. Francesca the Football Fairy ☐
59. Zoe the Skating Fairy ☐
60. Naomi the Netball Fairy ☐
61. Samantha the Swimming Fairy ☐
62. Alice the Tennis Fairy ☐
63. Gemma the Gymnastics Fairy ☐

The Music Fairies
64. Poppy the Piano Fairy ☐
65. Ellie the Guitar Fairy ☐
66. Fiona the Flute Fairy ☐
67. Danni the Drum Fairy ☐
68. Maya the Harp Fairy ☐
69. Victoria the Violin Fairy ☐
70. Sadie the Saxophone Fairy ☐

The Magical Animal Fairies

71. Ashley the Dragon Fairy ☐
72. Lara the Black Cat Fairy ☑
73. Erin the Firebird Fairy ☐
74. Rihanna the Seahorse Fairy ☐
75. Sophia the Snow Swan Fairy ☐
76. Leona the Unicorn Fairy ☑
77. Caitlin the Ice Bear Fairy ☐

The Green Fairies

78. Nicole the Beach Fairy ☑
79. Isabella the Air Fairy ☑
80. Edie the Garden Fairy ☐
81. Coral the Reef Fairy ☑
82. Lily the Rainforest Fairy ☐
83. Carrie the Snow Cap Fairy ☐
84. Milly the River Fairy ☑

The Ocean Fairies

85. Ally the Dolphin Fairy ☐
86. Amelie the Seal Fairy ☐
87. Pia the Penguin Fairy ☐
88. Tess the Sea Turtle Fairy ☑
89. Stephanie the Starfish Fairy ☐
90. Whitney the Whale Fairy ☐
91. Courtney the Clownfish Fairy ☐

The Twilight Fairies

92. Ava the Sunset Fairy ☐
93. Lexi the Firefly Fairy ☐
94. Zara the Starlight Fairy ☐
95. Morgan the Midnight Fairy ☐
96. Yasmin the Night Owl Fairy ☐
97. Maisie the Moonbeam Fairy ☐
98. Sabrina the Sweet Dreams Fairy ☐

The Showtime Fairies

99. Madison the Magic Show Fairy ☑
100. Leah the Theatre Fairy ☐
101. Alesha the Acrobat Fairy ☐
102. Darcey the Dance Diva Fairy ☐
103. Taylor the Talent Show Fairy ☐
104. Amelia the Singing Fairy ☑
105. Isla the Ice Star Fairy ☐

The Princess Fairies

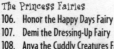

106. Honor the Happy Days Fairy ☐
107. Demi the Dressing-Up Fairy ☐
108. Anya the Cuddly Creatures Fairy ☐
109. Elisa the Adventure Fairy ☐
110. Lizzie the Sweet Treats Fairy ☑
111. Maddie the Playtime Fairy ☐
112. Eva the Enchanted Ball Fairy ☐

The Pop Star Fairies

113. Jessie the Lyrics Fairy ☑
114. Adele the Singing Coach Fairy ☐
115. Vanessa the Dance Steps Fairy ☑
116. Miley the Stylist Fairy ☐
117. Frankie the Make-Up Fairy ☐
118. Rochelle the Star Spotter Fairy ☐
119. Una the Concert Fairy ☐

The Fashion Fairies

120. Miranda the Beauty Fairy ☐
121. Claudia the Accessories Fairy ☐
122. Tyra the Dress Designer Fairy ☐
123. Alexa the Fashion Reporter Fairy ☐
124. Matilda the Hair Stylist Fairy ☑
125. Brooke the Photographer Fairy ☐
126. Lola the Fashion Fairy ☐

The Sweet Fairies

127. Lottie the Lollipop Fairy ☐
128. Esme the Ice Cream Fairy ☐
129. Coco the Cupcake Fairy ☐
130. Clara the Chocolate Fairy ☐
131. Madeleine the Cookie Fairy ☐
132. Layla the Candyfloss Fairy ☐
133. Nina the Birthday Cake Fairy ☑

The Baby Animal Rescue Fairies

134. Mae the Panda Fairy ☐
135. Kitty the Tiger Fairy ☐
136. Mara the Meerkat Fairy ☐
137. Savannah the Zebra Fairy ☐
138. Kimberley the Koala Fairy ☐
139. Rosie the Honey Bear Fairy ☐
140. Anna the Arctic Fox Fairy ☐

The Magical Crafts Fairies

141. Kayla the Pottery Fairy ☐
142. Annabelle the Drawing Fairy ☐
143. Zadie the Sewing Fairy ☐
144. Josie the Jewellery-Making Fairy ☑
145. Violet the Painting Fairy ☐
146. Libby the Story-Writing Fairy ☐
147. Roxie the Baking Fairy ☐

There's a book of fairy fun for everyone!

www.rainbowmagicbooks.co.uk

Lila & Myla the Twins Fairies

Meet Lila and Myla the Twins Fairies!
Can the fairies stop Jack Frost before he uses
their magic to create his very own twin?

www.rainbowmagicbooks.co.uk